Contents

I am a dentist 4

Arriving at work 6

Team meeting 8

Getting ready 10

My first patient 12

Family appointment 14

Wobbly tooth 16

Getting a brace 18

False teeth 20

Going home 22

Glossary 23

Index 24

I am a dentist

My name is Joe.
I am a dentist.

This is where I work.
It is called the Lawley
Dental **Practice**.

DENTIST

Rebecca Hunter

Photography by
Chris Fairclough

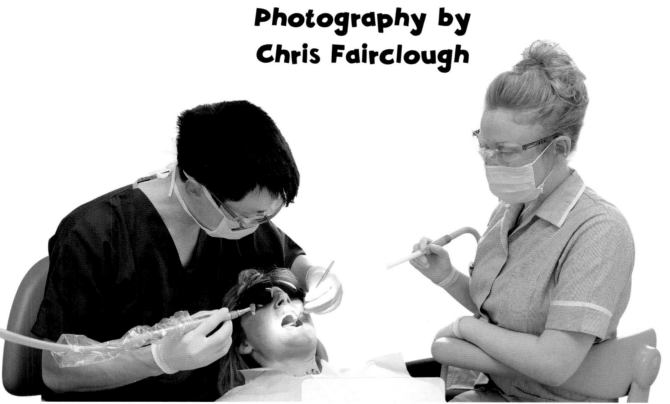

MILLENNIUM

TULIP BOOKS®

www.tulipbooks.co.uk

This edition published by:
  Tulip Books
  Dept 302
  43 Owston Road
  Carcroft
  Doncaster
  DN6 8DA.

The author would like to thank Joe Wong, Mike Prendergas, the staff and patients of the Lawley Dental Practice and Maddie and Gabriel Wong for their participation in this book.

Acknowledgements
Commissioned photography by Chris Fairclough.

British Library Cataloguing in Publication Data (CIP) is available for this title.

ISBN: 978-1-78388-018-8

Printed in Spain by Edelvives

Words appearing in bold **like this**, are explained in the glossary.

At eight o'clock I leave home. Before I go to work I have to take my daughter to school and my son to his nursery.

Arriving at work

I arrive at the **practice** at about half past eight. I let myself in with my key.

I say hello to Anne our **receptionist** and Laura, one of our dental nurses.

At this time of day they are busy taking phone calls.

This is my **partner** Carl. He is also a dentist.
We run the practice together.

Team meeting

Every morning we hold a team meeting. Denise, the **practice** manager, tells us some of the things that will be happening during the day.

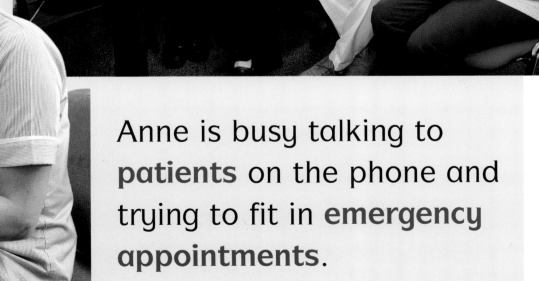

Anne is busy talking to **patients** on the phone and trying to fit in **emergency appointments**.

The waiting room is filling up with patients. There are lots of magazines and comics for them to read while they wait. There are also toys for the children to play with.

Getting ready

In my **surgery**, I turn on my computer. On the computer I can check the **records** of the **patients** I am about to see.

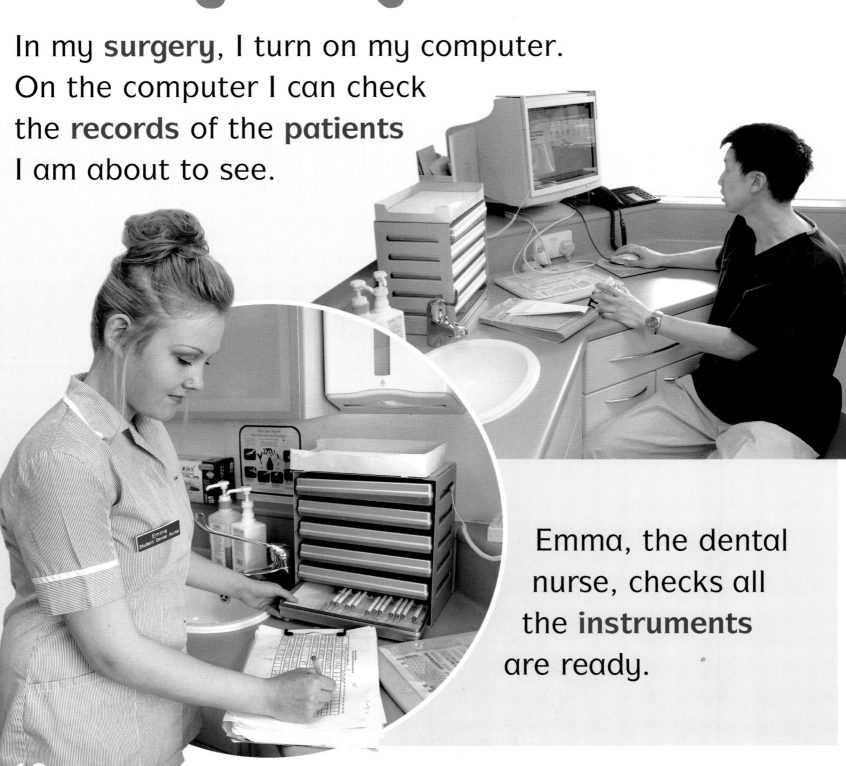

Emma, the dental nurse, checks all the **instruments** are ready.

Some of the instruments are in the autoclave.
This is a machine that **sterilizes** instruments
by heating them up with very hot
steam. Emma gets them out.

I need to ask Carl a
question, so I pop
into his surgery.

He is having a meeting with Sheena,
who has just **qualified** as a dentist.

My first patient

My first **patient** today is Rebecca. She has come in for a check-up.

Denise shows her into my room.

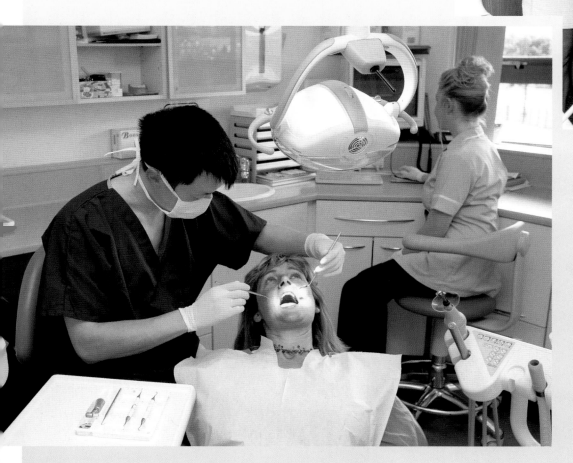

I put on my mask and some gloves. Rebecca wears a bib to protect her clothes.

I check Rebecca's teeth for signs of **decay**. But they are in good condition so I just clean them with my polishing brush. She has to wear glasses for this, to protect her eyes.

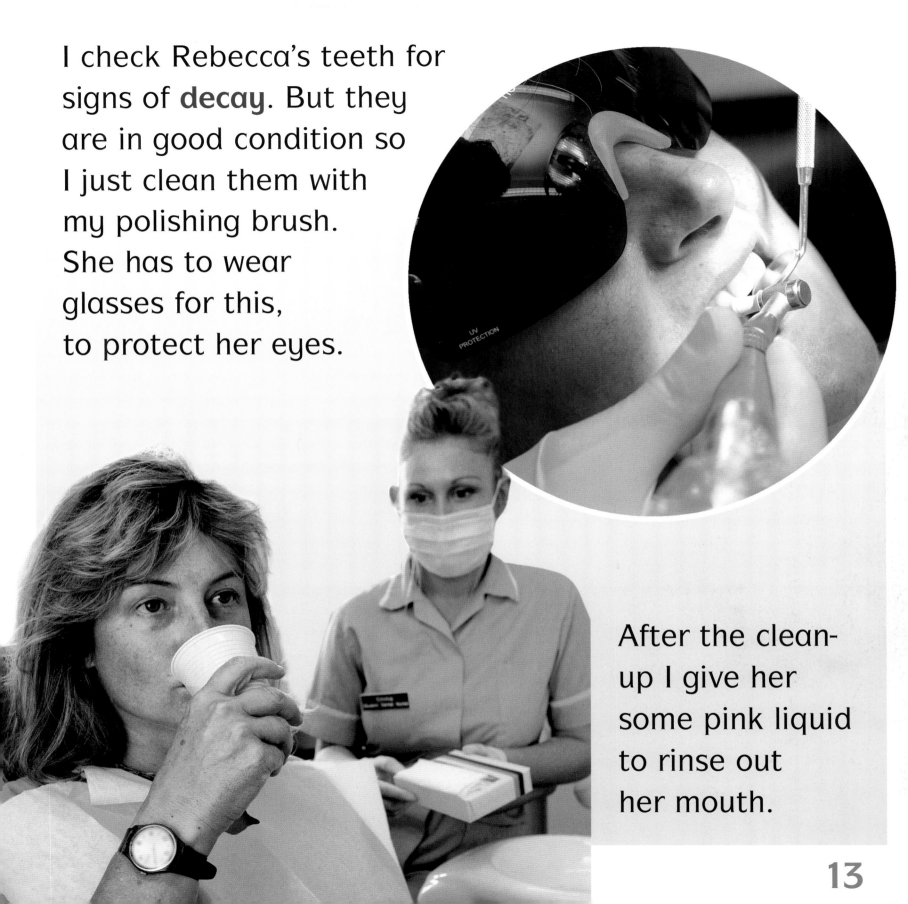

After the clean-up I give her some pink liquid to rinse out her mouth.

Family appointment

Sally has just moved to this area. She has brought her three children in to **register** them at the **practice**. Denise gives her a form to fill in about the children's **medical history**.

I have a quick look at the children's teeth. I tell them how important it is to brush their teeth properly.

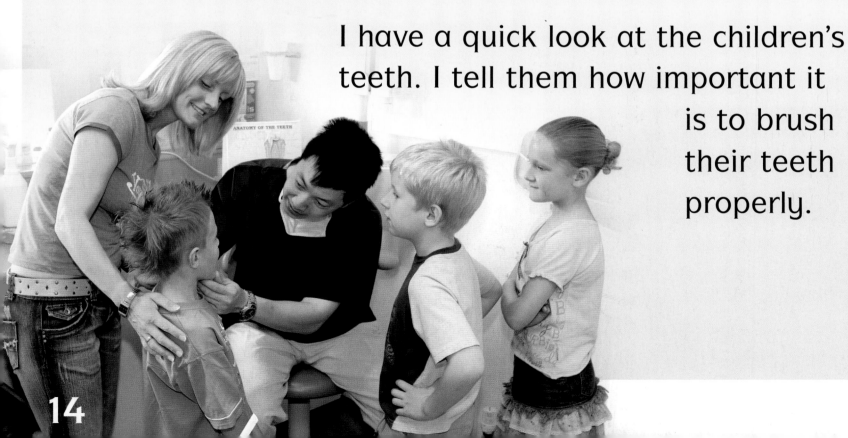

I show Megan my dentist's chair. She has fun seeing how it goes up and down and can tilt backwards.

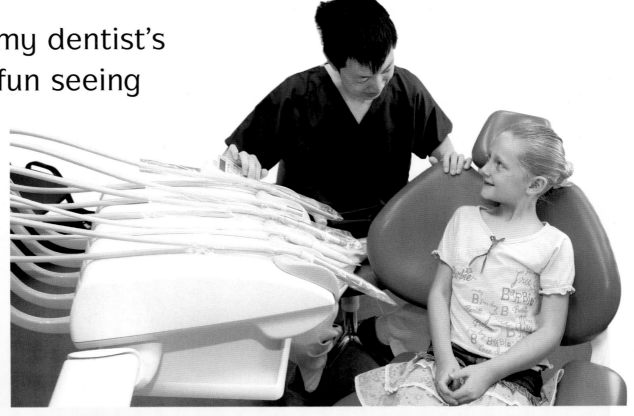

Before the children go, Emma the nurse gives them all a sticker.

15

Wobbly tooth

Maddie has a wobbly tooth. It won't come out and it hurts when she tries to eat. I put some cream on her gum so it won't hurt. Then I pull the tooth out quickly.

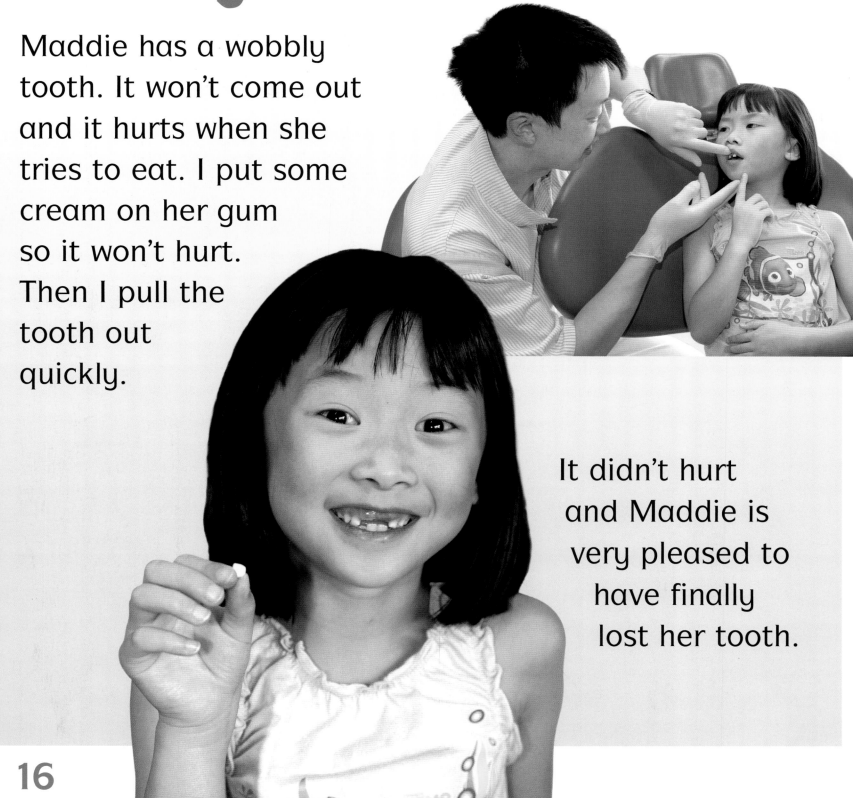

It didn't hurt and Maddie is very pleased to have finally lost her tooth.

I have had a busy morning. Before lunch I do some work. I need to write some letters and make some phone calls. I will have time to eat my sandwiches before my next **appointment**.

Getting a brace

William may need a **brace** to straighten his teeth. I have a look at his mouth.

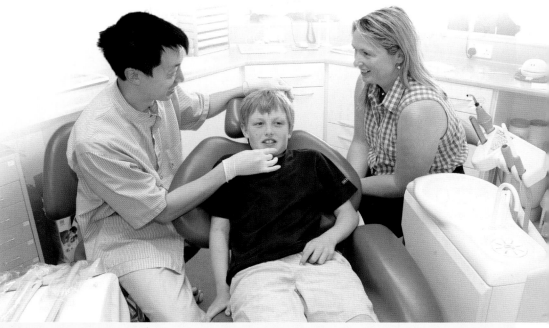

I take William into our **X-ray** room. This machine will take an X-ray of his teeth.

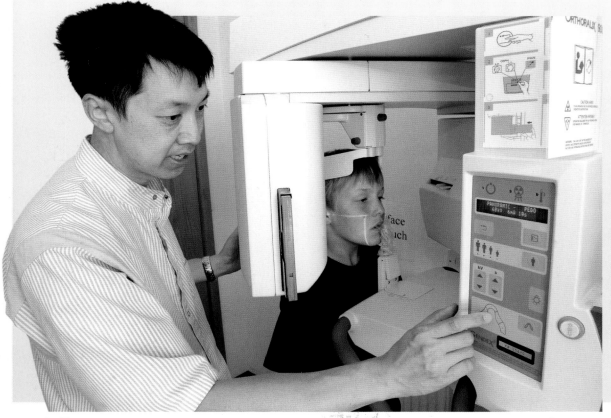

Here is the X-ray of William's teeth. I can see that his teeth will need straightening. He will have to wear a brace.

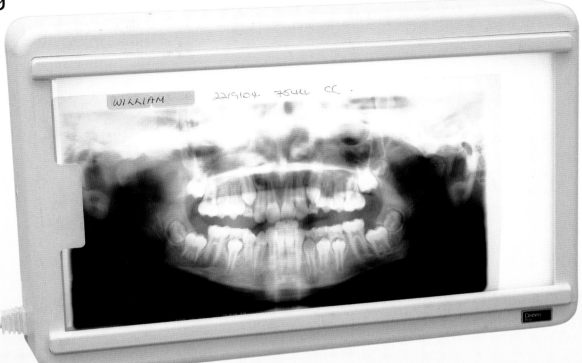

I show him some pictures of what it will look like. He will need to go and see the **orthodontist**.

False teeth

In reception, Vicky, a **dental technician**, is delivering some new **dentures**. The dentures are for my next **patient** Pat.

He lost all his teeth through **decay** many years ago. His dentures are very old now. They are quite worn out.

Dentures make a big difference to people who have lost all their own teeth.

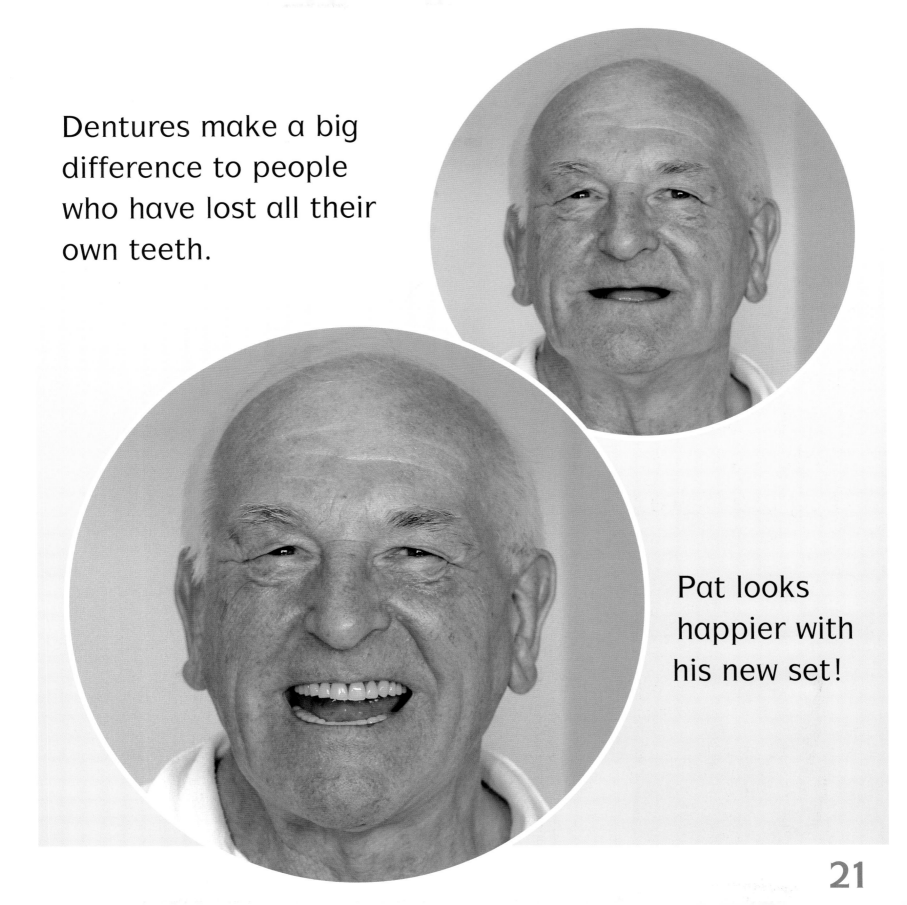

Pat looks happier with his new set!

Going home

It has been a busy day and I have seen about 30 **patients**. I love my job but I am glad when it is time to go home.

I collect my jacket and say goodbye to Beryl our cleaner who is cleaning up the coffee room.

Glossary

appointment an arranged time for a meeting with someone

brace a wire fitting worn across the teeth to straighten them

decay when something begins to rot or breaks up

dental technician someone who makes dentures for a dentist

dentures false teeth

emergency a serious situation that must be dealt with immediately

instrument a tool for delicate work

medical history the story of the treatment a patient has received from a dentist or doctor

orthodontist a dentist who deals with crooked teeth

partners people who run a business together

patients the people who visit a dentist or doctor

practice the place of work for a dentist, doctor or lawyer

qualify to pass exams

receptionist the person who welcomes visitors, answers the telephone and arranges appointments

records a list of what has happened to somebody

register to put your name down on a list

sterilize to make something really clean by killing all the germs

surgery the room where dentists and doctors see patients

X-ray invisible rays that make special pictures of your bones or teeth

Index

appointments 8, 17
autoclave 11

brace 18, 19

check-ups 12, 14
children 5, 9, 14, 15, 16, 18, 19
computer 10, 17

decay 13
dental nurse 10, 11, 13, 15
dental technician 20
dentist's chair 15
dentures 20, 21

false teeth 20, 21

instruments 10, 11

meetings 8, 11

orthodontist 19

partner 7
patient records 10
phone calls 6, 8, 17
polishing teeth 13
practice 4, 6, 7
practice manager 8

receptionist 6
registering 14
rinsing 13

sterilizing 11
stickers 15
surgery 10

waiting room 9
wobbly tooth 16

X-rays 18, 19